If all the world were...

For everyone who misses someone – JC

To dearest Sunday,
and thank you, Zoë – AC

Brimming with creative inspiration, how-to projects, and useful information to enrich your everyday life, Quarto Knows is a favourite destination for those pursuing their interests and passions. Visit our site and dig deeper with our books into your area of interest: Quarto Creates, Quarto Cooks, Quarto Homes, Quarto Lives, Quarto Drives, Quarto Explores, Quarto Gifts, or Quarto Kids.

Text © 2018 Joseph Coelho. Illustrations © 2018 Allison Colpoys.
First published in 2018 by Lincoln Children's Books, an imprint of The Quarto Group,
The Old Brewery, 6 Blundell Street, London N7 9BH, United Kingdom.
T (0)20 7700 6700 F (0)20 7700 8066 www.QuartoKnows.com
This paperback edition published 2019

ISBN 978-1-78603-651-3

Illustrated digitally
Designed by Zoë Tucker
Edited by Kate Davies
Published by Katie Cotton
Commissioned by Rachel Williams
Production by Catherine Cragg

Manufactured in Dongguan, China TL102018
9 8 7 6 5 4 3 2 1

MIX
Paper from
responsible sources
FSC® C104723

If all the world were...

Joseph Coelho
& Allison Colpoys

Frances Lincoln
First Editions

It's spring.

I take long walks with my grandad.
I hold his giant hand.
He says, "You're too old to hold hands."

We explore,

hand in hand,

the budding springtime.

If all the world were springtime,
I would replant my grandad's birthdays
so that he would never get old.

It's summer.

Grandad buys me a racing track.
It's second-hand with missing bits.
We fix what we can together.

We use our hands to
zoom the cars up and down,

up and down,

up, up, up
and fire them off
into deep space.

If all the world were deep space,
I'd orbit my grandad like the moon
and our laughs would be shooting stars.

It's autumn.

My grandad makes me a notebook
with handmade paper
of brown-and-orange leaves
that rustle when I turn the page,
bound with ruby Indian-leather string.

Grandad gives me a pencil
with a rainbow nib.

"Write and draw,

write and draw all
your dreams."

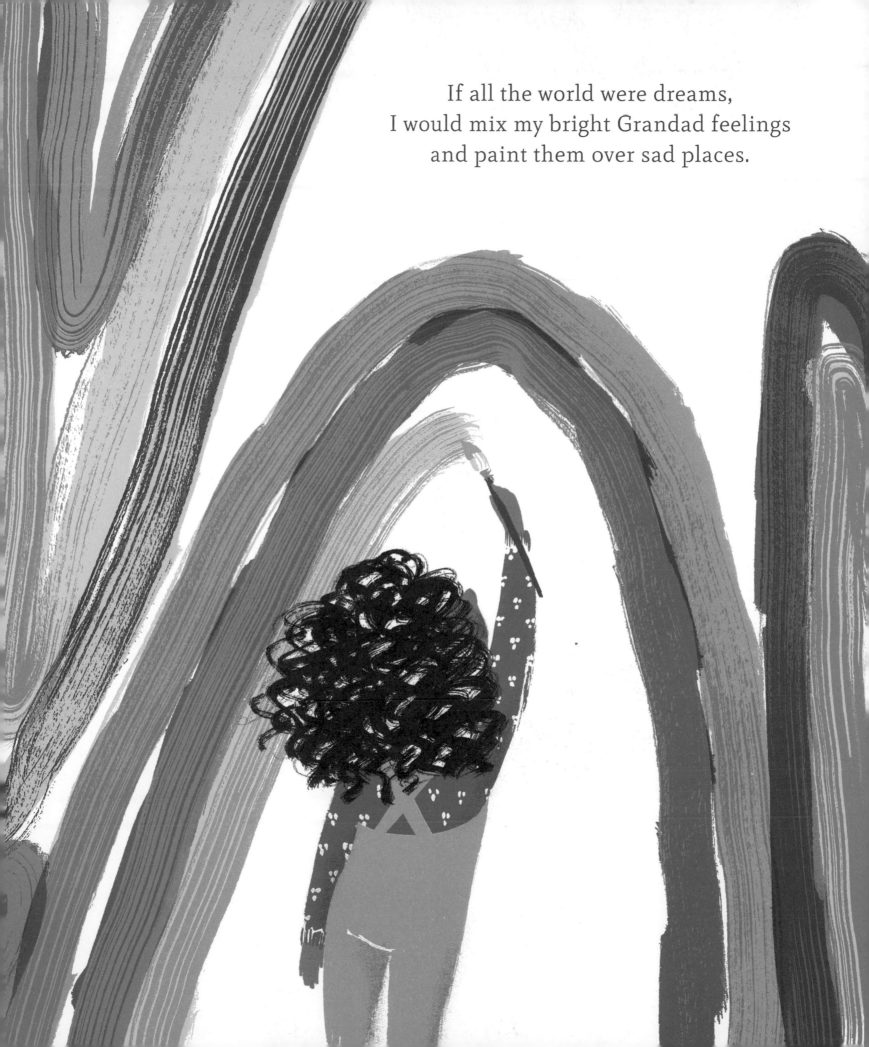

If all the world were dreams,
I would mix my bright Grandad feelings
and paint them over sad places.

It's winter.

My grandad tells me tales from when he was a boy,
of Indian sweets and homemade toys.

There are ships,

snakes

and tigers in his stories.

If all the world were stories,
I could make my grandad better
just by listening, listening, listening
to every tale he has to tell.

But some tales are silent.

I help Mum and Dad clean
out Grandad's room.

I find:
dried blue flowers between
book pages, a yellow toy racing car
glued to a piece of track, a length of
ruby Indian-leather string, a ball
of silver foil from every sweet
he ever ate, an open pack of
rainbow-nibbed pencils.

A kaleidoscope of memories.

If all the world were memories,
the past would be rooms I could visit
and in each room would be my grandad.

On Grandad's chair is a new notebook,
newly made with spring-petal paper,
newly bound with a length of Indian string.

My name is written on the front.
It's new and empty
and was made by my grandad.

So I write
and draw

and write and draw

and write
all my Grandad
memories inside.

I write and draw
lots of different worlds,

and all of them
have my grandad,

smiling
and laughing,
laughing,
laughing.

He says,
"You're too old to hold hands."

But still I hold his giant hand.
And we explore, hand in hand.